the Wind Wagon

BOOKS BY
CELIA BARKER LOTTRIDGE

Ticket to Curlew

ILLUSTRATED BY WENDY WOLSAK-FRITH

The Name of the Tree

ILLUSTRATED BY IAN WALLACE

Ten Small Tales

ILLUSTRATED BY JOANNE FITZGERALD

Something Might Be Hiding

ILLUSTRATED BY PAUL ZWOLAK

the Wind Wagon

by Celia Barker Lottridge

illustrated by Daniel Clifford

A Groundwood Book
Douglas & McIntyre * Vancouver / Toronto

For my father C.B.L.

*To my wife Loretta and
my children Anna and James* D.C.

Text © 1995 by Celia Barker Lottridge
Illustrations © 1995 by Daniel Clifford
Second Printing, 1995

First published in the United States by
Silver Burdett Press
A Simon and Schuster Company

Published in Canada by
Groundwood Books/Douglas & McIntyre Ltd.
585 Bloor Street West, Toronto, Ontario M6G 1K5

The publisher gratefully acknowledges the assistance of
the Canada Council, the Ontario Arts Council and the
Ontario Ministry of Culture, Tourism and Recreation.

Canadian Cataloguing in Publication Data

Lottridge, Celia B. (Celia Barker)
The wind wagon

ISBN 0-88899-234-3

1. Peppard, Sam—Juvenile fiction. I. Clifford, Daniel.
II. Title.
PS8573.0855W5 1995   jC813'.54   C95-930876-8
PZ7.L67Wi 1995

Designed by Sue Kyong Suk Brooks
Printed and bound in Canada by Webcom Ltd.

Chapter 1

SAM PEPPARD ARRIVED in the town of Oskaloosa on a summer day in 1859. The folks gossiping in front of the general store watched him jump down from the freight wagon that was making its regular stop with passengers and goods.

"There's another young fellow looking for a new life in Kansas Territory," said Joe Willard. Everybody laughed since Joe was a young fellow himself who had arrived not more than six months before.

Sam wasn't noticing the town folk, though. He was noticing the wind. It was a strong wind from the southwest, and it flattened Sam's denim shirt against his back and tried to lift his broad-brimmed hat off his head. Sam took a deep breath of the sweet smell of prairie grass and dust warmed by the sun.

"That's the smell of the West," said Joe. "Some folks get one whiff and travel on."

"Not me," said Sam. "I want to settle here." But there was a bit of regret in his eye as he watched the freight wagon rattle away. Then he got a grip on his hat and took a look at Oskaloosa.

He saw a few flat-fronted wooden buildings around a square that might, someday, have a courthouse in its center. The sidewalks were wooden, too, and the streets were dirt. Oskaloosa was a brand-new town just getting started in the rolling hills on the edge of the western plains.

"I reckon that this town needs a blacksmith," Sam said to Joe. He pointed to his bundle of tools. "That's good for me because I'm a blacksmith. I like this place. It's right on the edge of the east and the west and the north and the south. Someday it will be dead center of this country—just where I want to be."

So Sam opened up a smithy on the north side of the square, next to the livery stable. He was right. Oskaloosa did need a blacksmith to make wagon-wheel rims and nails and hinges and to shoe horses and mules. Besides, folks needed a place to hang around and talk, and Sam's shop suited them just fine. They would stand around the forge and tell the latest news or listen to Sam's stories about his travels.

Sam lived in a room behind his shop. Every morning before he opened up he would step out the front door and test the wind. If it blew from the north, south, or west, he

would step right back in and start to work. But if the wind was from the east, he would stand facing west in the middle of the street and stretch his arms out while the wind whipped his shirttails around his ears.

Folks got used to the sight, but they teased Sam about it. Some said, "You be careful, Sam. That wind is gonna blow you straight to Denver someday."

"I'd rather go by wind than by oxcart," Sam would say.

The country around Oskaloosa was a jumping-off place for people traveling west. Just north ran the Oregon Trail and just south ran the Santa Fe Trail. But whatever trail people took, they all went by oxcart. Prairie schooners, they were called, and they lumbered over the flat prairie at a mighty slow rate.

Sam thought about all those miles of waving prairie grass. "If that was water, with real schooners sailing before the wind, it would be a pretty sight," he said to Joe.

"It's a beautiful thought," said Joe, grinning, "only there isn't any water."

"There's plenty of wind, though," said Sam and he began to make a plan.

One winter day the folks who made a habit of warming themselves beside Sam's smithy fire found him building something. It looked like a wagon box. Funny shape, though, kind of narrow.

"Eight feet long, three feet wide," Sam said when they asked him about it, but he wouldn't explain why he was building it.

He wouldn't explain why the wheels were so high either or why the metal rims were so thick. When they asked him why he was fiddling around with some contraption at the rear of the wagon and where the horse or the ox was going to be hitched, Sam just said, "This isn't a horsecart or an oxcart. You'll see."

One morning, Joe went into Sam's shop and found Sam fixing something that looked very much like a mast in the front of the wagon. "Exactly what *is* this thing you're building?" he said. "Are you aiming to put a sail to a wagon?"

"Joe," said Sam, "I'm aiming to use the wind. There's more wind than anything else out there on the prairie. It blows east. It blows west. It blows north and south. Why can't it take folks along with it? Think of it, Joe—sails across the prairie."

Joe shook his head, but he caught a little of what Sam was seeing. "You gonna call it a sailing wagon?"

"A wind wagon. That's what it is—a wind wagon," said Sam Peppard.

Chapter 2

BY TEN O'CLOCK that morning, news of Sam's outlandish wagon was all over town. By noon, nearly everyone who could walk had come by to look at it. Most had quite a bit to say to Sam, generally along the lines of, "Sam, you're crazier than we thought you were."

Some people got around to asking him, "And just where are you planning to go in that thing?"

"Denver," said Sam. "I've heard they've made silver strikes in the mountains up behind Denver. I figure the wind wagon would be the best way to get there."

"Denver's six hundred miles!"

"There's wind all the way," said Sam.

After that, Sam got hardly a minute's peace. Sociable as he was, he got pretty tired of admitting he might be crazy, but nevertheless, he was headed for Denver.

Not everybody thought the wind wagon was a joke. Joe decided to go with Sam. "I've taken a pretty good look at that wagon of yours," he said. "I don't see how you can manage the sail and that steering stick at the same time. I'll come along and give you a helping hand."

"That stick is called a tiller," said Sam. "And I'm glad you'll be coming along."

Mary Alice Bellows, a townswoman, said she would make the sail. "A blacksmith you may be, Sam Peppard, and a carpenter too. But I expect there are some things you can't do," she said.

Sam had been thinking about the master sailmakers he had seen back east. He knew they had a skill in their fingers that he didn't have. He accepted Mary Alice's offer. "I thank you kindly, Miz Bellows. I'll bring you a silver locket," he said to her.

One afternoon when Sam was getting ready to close up shop, he looked up and saw a thin gray man with a weather-beaten face watching him silently from the doorway. Sam had seen him a time or two before and knew that the old man farmed a claim to the west of Oskaloosa. "Howdy, oldtimer," Sam said.

The old man just stared at the wind wagon for a long moment. At last he spoke. "Thought you ought to know, my shack blew away."

"Too bad," said Sam.

"Cow, too."

Sam said nothing.

"Wind's mighty strong out there."

There was a long pause. "My wind wagon is made to go with the wind."

There was a longer pause. "There's 'go with,' " said the old man to Sam, "and then there's 'blown away'. Can't see there's much difference."

After that the old-timer would come and stand in the doorway every day or two, staring at the wind wagon and shaking his head. Sam ignored him as best he could. The wind wagon was almost ready to go, and he was busy getting his regular work finished up. As he worked, he stopped now and then to add a little touch to the wind wagon. He painted *Wind Wagon*, *Oskaloosa* on the back panel. He polished up the brass fittings of the mast. He greased the big iron wheels until they turned sweetly, without a murmur of complaint.

One day, Joe dropped by. "I've been thinking, Sam," he said. "The two of us aren't going to be enough. There's a lot to do—

managing the sail, steering, keeping a look-out for trouble, gathering buffalo chips so we can have a fire, cooking, shooting rabbits to eat. We'll be too tired to go looking for silver when we get to Denver."

"Who did you have in mind?" asked Sam.

"What about the Graham boys? They don't talk much, and I reckon they're pretty good shots. One of them plays the banjo, too."

Sam knew the Graham boys, all right. They were the two most up-and-coming sons of a large family that lived on the edge of town. Their names were Abraham and Isaiah, but no one ever remembered which was which. They both were tall and lanky and silent, so they were just called the Graham boys.

"I don't guess they'd have got themselves steady jobs," said Sam. "I'll talk to them about it."

When he did, the boys looked at each other and allowed as how they weren't too busy this time of year and they wouldn't mind setting their eyes on the Rocky Mountains. But they did have one question. "Is that fool wagon of yours going to get us there for sure?" asked the Graham boys.

"The wind wagon will get us there," said Sam. "I'm just waiting for the right kind of wind to come along."

Chapter 3

ALL THE WIND that spring seemed to come from the west. Sam almost got discouraged. "There's one thing the wind wagon can't do, Joe," he said one day. "It can't sail into the wind. If it's blowing from the northeast or the southwest, we can just angle the sail a little and zigzag across the prairie. But if it's blowing straight out of the west, there's not much we can do."

One Saturday, Sam decided he couldn't wait any longer. The wind was still from the west, but it was so fresh and so sweet as he stood in the street and let it blow around him that he locked up the shop and went to look for Joe and the Graham boys.

"We've got to try the wind wagon out today," Sam told them. "I swear I can smell the snow melting in the high mountains and the flowers blooming in the foothills. One of these days the wind will be just right, and we've got to be ready to go."

So they hauled the wind wagon, by hand, to a big high piece of ground just north of town. It was about as flat as any place around Oskaloosa, but it had a steep slope at its east end.

"Perfect," said Sam. "Folks think the prairie is flat as a pancake, but we will definitely have to handle a few hills."

It was a tight squeeze in the wind wagon when they were all on board. One of the Graham boys said, "Don't know where you expect me to stick a banjo." But then Joe hoisted the sail and they were off.

Sam felt the wind in his hair. There was nothing ahead of the wagon—no horse, no ox—just the grassy field which seemed to pull itself under the wagon wheels smooth as silk. Well, not exactly. The wagon lurched and bumped along, and the Graham boys hung on for their lives, their faces white with fear, as if they might fall into a raging sea instead of Old Man Hicks's pasture.

All Sam could feel was the wind pushing the wind wagon along. The wind was solid. It was strong. It could push them all the way to Denver.

Some movement against the trees caught Sam's eye. He turned away from the on-rushing pasture and saw the old man from the claim. He was watching the wind wagon with fierce eyes, and Sam wondered for a second whether the old man wanted them to blow away or whether he hoped they wouldn't.

Just then the land sloped downward sharply. The wind was under the wagon's body. It was ballooning the sail and lifting the wind wagon off the ground. It occurred to Sam that the wind might blow them all the way to the Missouri River.

Then they were beyond the crest of the hill. The wind slackened and the wheels touched the earth again and bumped to a stop. After a minute they all got out and looked at the wind wagon. It was fine—no cracks, no bends.

"Well," said Sam, "this wagon takes to the wind. Give us a high enough hill and we might just take off. But I'll put a little ballast in front to keep the bow down and we'll stay on the ground, I guarantee." The Graham boys looked relieved.

The next day Sam was painting over a few scratches on the wagon box when he looked up to see the old-timer standing in the door-

way to the smithy. "You'd better get that thing fixed so that it stays on the ground," he said. "The wind's about to change."

For a minute Sam couldn't think of anything to say, which was unusual for him. But he collected himself. "We're ready," he said. "We'll make it to Denver—and back. I'll bring you a silver dollar."

But the old man shook his head. "Just keep that wagon on the ground," he said. "The wind out there . . . . "

The old man shook his head again. And then he was gone.

Chapter 4

THE WIND CHANGED the next day. It shifted from west to southwest, just enough to catch the wind wagon's sail and send them in the right direction. Sam wasted no time. He collected Joe and the Graham boys. They packed up the sourdough and beans they had ready, found a tight corner for the banjo and a deck of cards, and sent out the word that the wind wagon was ready to go.

Everyone in Oskaloosa showed up for the great send-off, except for a couple of skeptics who claimed Joe, Sam, and the Graham boys would be home by sundown, on foot. The old-timer didn't miss it. He stood at the back of the crowd, slowly shaking his head.

Sam paid him no attention. He stood up in the back of the wind wagon, waved his broad-brimmed hand, and said, "Folks, if you wanted to beat us to Denver, you should have started off three weeks ago." Then he sat down, set his hat squarely on his head to shade his eyes from the brilliant sun, and took hold of the tiller.

Joe pulled the sail around until the wind caught it, and several boys ran alongside the wagon to give it a push. And then the wind wagon, creaking a little, sailed off along the ridge road leading west out of town.

Three long days later they reached the edge of the Flint Hills where the land quits rolling and levels out into a five-hundred-mile slow upward incline to the Rocky Mountains. Before them lay the hard-packed road to

Denver, rutted and worn by the wheels of all the wagons that had carried people looking for land or gold or silver near Denver. In the distance they could see quite a swarm of prairie schooners lurching along.

"Come on, boys," said Sam Peppard, "we'll catch 'em before the sun is high!" He stretched his arms out as wide as he could and felt the strong prairie wind pulling at his shirtsleeves.

And so the great wind wagon voyage began. Sam had his accustomed place in the back of the wagon, handling the tiller. The others took turns looking after the sail and keeping lookout for buffalo or antelope or a fat prairie chicken to eat for dinner.

For the first week or so, the wind blew strong and steady. The wind wagon rolled along, overtaking wagons that moved slowly to the pace of a team of oxen. Sam loved to wait for the moment when people riding in those wagons heard the clatter of the wind

wagon and turned to stare in amazement at a wagon with a tall white sail and nothing pulling it. Then he would politely touch the brim of his hat as the wind wagon rattled past.

On the ninth day the wind died down. The folks in some of the slow, steady, ox-drawn wagons had the satisfaction of seeing the wind wagon drawn off the trail while its crew played cards and hunted rabbits. The people weren't very polite about it, either. "Never mind," said Sam. "They'll be eating our dust soon enough."

And Sam was right. When the wind blew again, it was fresher and stronger than ever. Sam, Joe, and the Graham boys soon pulled past the main body of wagons and had the road to themselves. For a good number of days the wind wagon rolled along so fast and so smoothly that even the Graham boys had to admit that it looked like they would live to see the Rocky Mountains.

On one of those days, Sam said, "I'd wager we're going twenty-five miles an hour." Since neither Joe nor the Graham boys had any notion about the wind wagon's speed— except knowing that they were going mighty fast—they didn't argue with Sam. But one of the Graham boys, who happened to have the side lookout spot, said, "Then I sure hope those Indians can't ride twenty-five miles an hour."

They all looked up and, sure enough, there were three Indians on spotted horses riding at a gallop in their direction. Now, Sam hoped he had never done anything to make any Indians sore at him, but he knew that a lot of Indians had a lot to be sore about, so he wasn't sure these Indians had friendly thoughts. And they were certainly coming on fast.

"Come on, wind wagon," he said, "now's the time to show what you can do." All the men hunkered down to give the sail a chance to do the most it could, while Sam fiddled with the tiller.

Joe lifted his head above the edge of the sideboards and said, "By gum, Sam, I think they're racing us."

Sam, Joe, and the Graham boys saw the Indians were riding about a hundred yards to the south of the wind wagon and about fifty yards back. Sam grinned. "Well, they've got themselves a race," he said.

The wind was with them that day. After about ten miles of hard riding, the Indians were getting closer but they were still behind the wind wagon. At last the Indians shouted something to each other, waved their arms in a friendly fashion, and turned south. That night, Sam went to sleep knowing that the wind wagon could surely go like the wind.

And the wind kept getting stronger and stronger as the land rose toward the Rockies. On some days they didn't raise the sail all the way up. "Either it will get blown to

rags, or that wind will take us right up into the air," said Sam. As he said it, he remembered the old-timer and thought, "It's just too bad that being blown away can't get you where you're going."

Chapter 5

ON THE MORNING of their twenty-second day on the road Sam studied the map while he drank his coffee. "I reckon we're just about eighty miles from Denver," he said. They were all feeling pretty good. Three weeks to Denver was mighty good time, especially considering the five or six days when they had done nothing but play cards and hunt rabbits.

Of course, the Graham boys were beginning to fret about the Rocky Mountains.

They could see the mountains already, looking like a solid cloud on the horizon. "They must be mighty high," one of the Graham boys said. "What if we fall off?"

Sam was a bit agitated himself as he got settled by the tiller, but he figured it was because he hated to come to the end of the wind wagon's first voyage.

He looked at the sky and thought they should have a good run. There were some dark clouds to the southwest, but the sky up ahead was clear blue and the wind had calmed down some. As the wagon picked up speed, Sam settled back and began to wonder how they were going to convince the people back in Oskaloosa that the wind wagon had really made it to Denver.

Suddenly an immense gust of wind hit the wind wagon broadside. The whole wagon shivered violently. At the same moment, Joe hollered, "It's a twister!"

Sam looked where Joe was pointing. Coming out of the southwest was a thin black finger of wind, twisting and snaking its way straight at the wind wagon, roaring like a thousand bulls spooked by thunder.

Sam gripped the tiller tightly. It seemed as if he should be able to dodge something so narrow. But the twister was coming fast. Sam knew if that fierce wind wanted the wind wagon, there was nothing he could do about it now.

"Lower the sail," he yelled. And then, "Jump, boys!" But there wasn't time for anything. The twister swirled down upon the wind wagon and lifted it straight up into the air, with Sam hanging onto the tiller and the others holding tight to anything they could grab a hold of.

Sam felt the huge force of the wind as it held the wagon and him and Joe and the Graham boys twenty feet above the prairie.

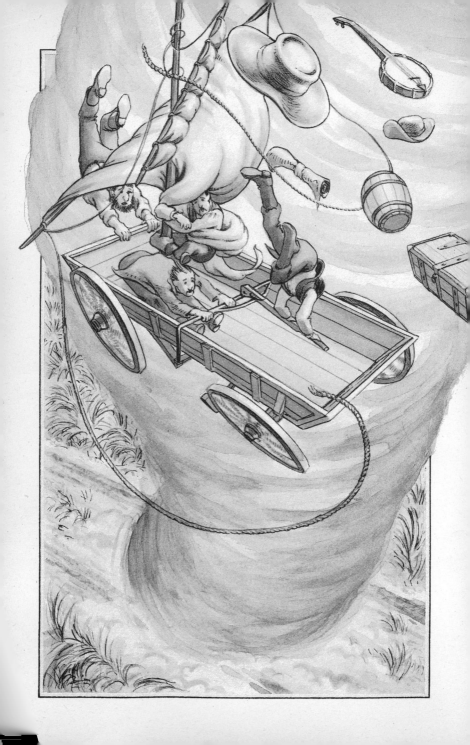

They hung in the air for so long Sam could have drawn a deep breath—if he had been thinking about breathing.

Then the twister dropped them, wind wagon and all, in a heap on the ground and went roaring away to the northeast.

It was a minute before Sam could see straight. The sudden silence felt strange to his ears, but he was all in one piece. He looked around at his crew. They didn't seem to be hurt. Joe was slowly shaking his head and the Graham boys were cautiously moving their arms and legs. But the wind wagon was in a thousand pieces.

Sam looked at the tangle of sail and the splintered boards and bent wheels. "Well, boys," he said, "it looks like we walk the rest of the way." He finally took a deep breath. "But it sure was some ride while it lasted."

As it turned out, one of the lumbering freight wagons came along. With a few smirks and rude jokes, the driver offered them a ride into Denver. "Unless my team gets blowed away, of course," he said.

Sam just said, "Thank you kindly." But he remembered the power of that wind and knew that oxen could fly, too.

Joe found the back panel with the proud words *Wind Wagon, Oskaloosa* painted on it and handed it to Sam. It was hardly scratched. Sam put it under his arm. All the men climbed aboard the freight wagon and rode into Denver.

That's almost the end of the story. Sam, Joe, and the Graham boys did go silver mining before they hopped another wagon back to Oskaloosa. Sam brought home enough silver to build himself the little house and the lumber mill he'd been planning.

The old-timer showed up the day Sam stoked up the fire in his smithy. "You gonna build another of them wagons?" he asked. "Or have you had enough?"

"I'm not going to build another wind wagon," said Sam. "I'd never find a wind like I found the first time. I reckon I've gotten the most out of a wind wagon that I ever could. Some things are only meant to be done once. I'm going to settle down and stay put in Oskaloosa."

Sam did just that. He married, had ten children, and lived to be known for his long white beard. But he never forgot the wind wagon, especially when a strong wind blew from the southwest, bringing the smell of prairie grass and dust.

On such a day, Sam would gather his nearest grandchild to him and say, "Let me tell you a story about where that kind of wind took me. You might not believe it, but it's true. It's the story of the wind wagon. Just listen."